Especially Izi

Especially Izi

Stories of Mermaids, Momsters, and Magic

IZI MILLER

This one is for me :)

Text copyright © 2021 by Izi Miller

All rights reserved.
Published in the United States by Village Lane Publishing.

Visit us on the web!
www.VillageLanePublishing.com

Printed in the United States of America
First Edition

Free Short Story!

Enjoy short stories? Get another one for free!

Cassie Hillsdale isn't looking for a second chance at love. She's just looking to survive the bank robbery she finds herself in the middle of!

Scan below to download *Roses and Robberies*!

Contents

100 Gigabytes

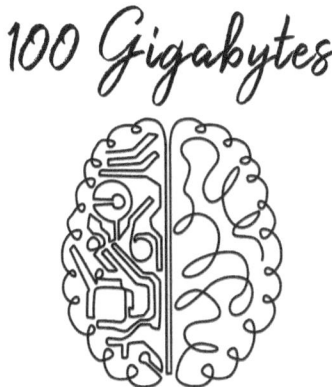

When I was born, my parents purchased the standard infant memory wetware package of 50 terabytes. Babies have to soak up a lot of new information, so you've got to start off with quite a bit of room in their brain or they'll turn out stupid. No one wants a stupid kid.

At three months, my parents upgraded my memory to a full 100 terabytes of wetware, giving me ample room to learn things like language and motor skills.

The human brain can hold up to 2.5 petabytes,

but the average person functions at 100 terabytes. Memory is $1 a gig. Since a terabyte is 1,000 gigabytes, and a petabyte is 1,000 terabytes, storage room in your brain gets a little pricey.

I might not be rich, but I certainly don't intend to be average. Since my sixteenth birthday, I've been working at a little burger and shake place on the corner of 9th and 27th. I make a nice $500 a month there, and mom lets me spend $100 of that on a H2735 100 gigabyte memory wetware package. I'm up to 1,600 gigabytes in my brain, and I don't intend to stop anytime soon.

The burger and shake place is where I first saw the tallest guy of my entire life. And by tallest I mean hottest. Because, let's be honest, at 5'11" I'm a disaster of a prom date. Tall equals attractive. As long as he isn't stupid. Obviously.

This guy was wearing a t-shirt that said, "There are 10 types of people in this world: those who understand binary numbers and those who don't." So he fell into the hot category.

While he was standing in line, I kept thinking, "Please come to my cash register!" But when he did, my brain shut off. It was like all those gigabytes I had in my skull got unplugged, and I couldn't remember how to even smile.

"Hey, Sienna," he said.

This guy knew me?! I forgot how to breathe too.

"We missed you at Todd's on Friday," he said. "Did you have to work?"

I guess my muscle memory kicked in because I said, "Would you like a shake with that?"

He laughed. "I'll take that as a yes."

I gave a nervous laugh back. James at the next cash register over gave me a weird look.

"You get off at 7:30 tonight?" the tall guy asked.

He also knew my schedule? It would have been creepy if he wasn't so tall and nerdy.

I managed to nod.

"Want to see a movie or something?"

Was he asking me out? I said, "Uh…."

He laughed again, only this time it sounded a little concerned. "You okay?" he asked.

I nodded again.

Glancing over his shoulder, he saw the dinner line stacking up. "I'll text you."

I nodded again. Once I had remembered how to do something I couldn't stop doing it.

"'Kay," he said. "See you later?"

I nodded for the hundredth time.

He gave me a hesitant smile on his way out the door. I nodded back.

"You sure you're alright?" James asked, leaning over to me.

"What?" Now that the tall guy was out of sight, my brain rebooted. "Yeah, of course."

James raised his eyebrows.

At 7:30, two hours after the tall-guy encounter, I clocked out and checked my phone. There was a text. I didn't recognize the name, but my phone knew the number.

Keene: You up for a movie tonight?

If I had entered this guy's number into my phone I had to know who he was, right? When I opened the text, there wasn't just one message. There were dozens of previous conversations. More than I could scroll back through. Clutching the phone, I stared at the black letters against the glowing screen, at all these old texts I could not remember sending or receiving.

Keene: Morning sunshine :)

Me: Morning handsome :)

Me: I got the sticky note you left on my locker. Did you have to skip school to do that? You're the sweetest!

Keene: <3

Me: Happy three-month anniversary!! :*

Keene: Best three months of my life! :D

Keene: P.S. Have I told you you're gorgeous?

Me: Have I told you you're the best boyfriend ever?

I finally got to the beginning of the texts, three whole months earlier.

My phone rang making me jump. The caller ID said it was Keene.

I answered automatically. "Hello?"

"Hey, Sienna!" It was the tall guy. He sounded relieved. "How was work?"

"It was fine." My breath was making misty air in front of me. He had my number. Was he a stalker? He seemed geeky and attractive, which I was all for, but how had he gotten my number? How had I gotten his?

"Great!" he said. "So, are you up for a movie tonight? Or do you want to get home early to study for the competition tomorrow?"

"A movie sounds nice. I like movies." What was I saying? Words were just coming out of my mouth. How did he know I had a math competition tomorrow? "But I'd better ask my mom."

"Oh," he said. "Sure. I mean, do you guys have something going on this evening?"

"No," I said. "No, we don't. I don't think we do. I just don't want her to worry."

"Okay," he said. "Yeah. Of course. Let me know?"

"Yeah." My voice was too high. "Yeah, I'll text you."

"Okay," he said. "Talk to you soon."

I nodded, which was stupid. He couldn't see me.

"Hey, Sienna?"

"Yeah?"

He paused for a second. "Are we okay?"

"What?"

"You and me? Are we... you know, okay?"

"Uh..." My brain was rifling through all 1,600 gigabytes of memory storage, trying to dig up something on this guy. I pictured papers flying as little people inside my head tore through filing cabinets full of folders of information on my life. I was coming up blank.

"It's okay," he said. "You don't have to answer that. We can talk about it later. Let me know if you want to do something tonight."

"Yeah."

"Love you." He disconnected.

I held the phone to my ear for a few blank seconds. Then I sat down on the curb so hard my butt hurt. I was crazy. That was the only explanation. My phone thought I'd had a boyfriend for over three months. Either the phone was crazy or I was. I typed

6

out a text to my mom. I didn't want to admit I might be losing my mind, but I needed some sort of confirmation from her that I wasn't hallucinating this guy. I debated what to say for a few minutes before texting her.

Me: A guy named Keene asked me to go to the movies tonight. Is that alright?

I took slow breaths in through my nose and out through my mouth while I waited for her to text back. My sanity depended on her reply. But when my phone chimed, all I had was a winky face. What was that supposed to mean?

I rubbed my arms and looked up and down the street. I usually walked home, but if there was a chance I might be going on a date instead, I didn't want to pass up the opportunity. I wondered if that made me stupid. I guess no matter how much brain capacity you have at birth, it doesn't guarantee you'll make smart decisions.

Texting Keene back took way too long since I deleted the text at least five times.

Me: My mom doesn't mind. Movie?

Keene: Great! I'll be there in five.

Shoving the phone in my pocket, I huddled on the cement and waited. I wondered if this was a prank my friends were pulling to see if they could hook me up. Or if this guy was a serial killer who had stolen my phone for a bit before approaching me. Maybe my body would show up on the news tomorrow. There had to be some software to load fake texts onto a phone, right?

A beat-up brown truck pulled up to the curb next to me and the window rolled down.

"Hey," Keene said.

"Hey," I said. I glanced at the license plate and committed it to memory, just in case. Good thing I had so much extra storage space. But I still got in the car, my heart jumping around.

"So," said Keene as we drove. "You want to talk about it?"

I fidgeted with my phone. "Uh..."

"You don't have to," he said. "But is it me? Am I doing something wrong?" When I still didn't answer, his knuckles whitened as he said, "Is there another guy?" He looked like he was strangling his steering wheel.

I gave a little laugh. "I'm a computer geek," I said. "What do you think?" Until five minutes ago, I hadn't thought there was even one guy.

He shrugged but didn't give his steering wheel a chance to breathe.

"If it's James," he said, "you should know-"

I burst out laughing. "James? Seriously? That guy is like an annoying little brother." I turned my phone screen on and then off again. My hands were still shaking.

"Then what is it?" He sounded angry.

"Is this a prank?" I asked.

His truck swerved as he turned to look at me. "What?"

"All of this," I said. "The texts, you showing up at my work, going to the movies- Did my friends put you up to this? I wouldn't put it past Camille to engineer something that could load customized texts onto a phone."

"What are you talking about?"

"You! I'm talking about you! This morning I was geeky and single and then you walked into the burger place and suddenly I've had a boyfriend for three months?"

He frowned and didn't answer until he'd pulled into the parking lot and turned off the car. "What's going on, Sienna?"

"That's what I'm trying to figure out!" I didn't bother unbuckling. "Who are you?"

Keene took in a slow breath. "Are you telling me you don't remember the last three months?"

"Of course I remember the last three months!

9

I have over a terabyte and a half of memory! I just don't remember you being a part of the last three months. In fact, I don't remember even seeing you before today!"

Keene ran his hands over the wheel, up the sides and back down again. "Is this a joke?"

"You're asking me?"

"I'm serious, Sienna!"

"So am I!" Our gazes locked.

His lips parted as he realized just how serious I was. I realized what a nice kissable look his lips had. I pressed my own lips together and looked away.

The interior of the car was starting to cool down now that the heater was off. I wished he would turn the car back on. I couldn't tell if my shaking was just the cold or something deeper.

"We've been together for three months, Sie," Keene said. His voice was low. "You've known me for six. My name is Keene Jay Anderson. I'm sixteen. My birthday is October 25th, almost three months before yours."

My shivering got stronger.

"I go to Seven Lakes High School on the other side of town from Kinaford High where you go to school. We met during the summer at a math competition. You creamed me."

"I remember the competition," I said. "I remember winning. But I don't remember you."

His eyes were an intense brown. They were the kind of eyes I loved - full of life and joy. I could see why I had fallen for him. If I actually had.

"I congratulated you afterwards," he said, "but really I just used that as an excuse to talk to this gorgeous girl who had just made all us guys look like idiots. I asked you for help with some math problems because I was too scared to ask you out. You gave me your number."

Massaging my forehead, I didn't ask the questions I was too embarrassed to ask. Have we kissed? You said, 'I love you' on the phone. Have I ever said it back? How serious are we?

"What was our first date?" I asked instead.

"We played laser tag."

That sounded plausible. "Did I win?"

He laughed. "You came in second."

"Okay, I might have believed you up until you said that. I always win at laser tag!"

"Ha! That's what you said when I asked you out. But you had never played against me." He smirked. It was adorable.

How many times had I seen that smirk? How many times that I had forgotten? If this was true, I had lost moments of my life. Moments I desperately wanted back.

I said, "Please tell me we had a rematch?"

"Of course! We've had several."

"And?"

"And you've won about half of them..."

"Half?"

He shrugged. "I'm telling you, I'm good."

I shook my head and looked out the window. "If this is real, why can't I remember it?"

"It is real," Keene said. "It's very real."

Lighting up my phone screen again, I typed in my pass code and opened the first social media app I could find. I needed more proof. My chest was starting to ache and I didn't want to grieve over losing something if it wasn't real.

There were pictures. Lots of pictures. So many that it would have taken someone ages to photoshop them all if they weren't genuine.

Pictures of Keene with his arms around me from behind.

Pictures of Keene and I taking selfies with laser guns.

Pictures of Keene kissing me.

I guess that answered that question. I could feel myself starting to blush.

Until I saw the ad on the side of the screen.

Recall notice: Memory product H2735 is being recalled due to corruptible wetware. If you have purchased this 100 GB memory product within the last seven months, free replacements are provided at most memory facilities. Talk to your local memory specialist for details.

I swallowed. It was real. All of it was real. A weight sunk onto my chest, the sorrow of losing three months of getting to know this handsome geek next to me.

"I think I just figured it out." I turned the phone screen toward him.

He read the ad with a few flicks of his eyes. Then his jaw tightened. "If we take you in for a replacement, do you think they could recover your memories? The ones you lost?"

I shook my head. "I doubt it. It says the wetware is being corrupted. I'm guessing all my memories of you were all sorted together. And something happened to that file in my brain."

"Are the memory centers still open?" he asked. "Where's the nearest place?"

I looked it up on my phone, but they were all closed for the evening.

"We can go tomorrow," I said.

He didn't respond.

"Hey," I said. "It's not that big of a deal." I could feel the lie as my voice caught. "I mean, I might not remember, but you can tell me everything. It's not the same, I know. But-"

He shook his head. "I bought some of those too," he said.

"Oh." We sat in silence, watching the streetlights as it began to snow.

"We should get home," I said. "Before the snow gets bad."

"Yeah." He didn't move.

I put my hand on his. It felt weird, reaching out to him, but once I touched him, my hand seemed to remember his even if my brain didn't. "It's okay," I said. "There's nothing to worry about. We can even skip school tomorrow if you want and go in first thing. They can exchange the memory on both of us. Transfer your files over."

"Yeah. Okay." He started the car.

Neither of us spoke the whole drive.

I woke up the next morning with a dull itch at the back of my mind. There was something I was going to do first thing in the morning. But I couldn't think what it was.

All I remembered was being exhausted when I climbed into bed last night, like my brain had done aerobic exercises.

When the school bus pulled up, I looked around before getting on, that niggling feeling turning into a headache. It was probably just the upcoming math competition.

I was 30 minutes early to the competition. I liked to stake out my competitors. There was the usual – lots of glasses and braces and a general lack of hygiene. All geniuses I was sure. All about to get creamed. But there was one guy that stood out, and not just because of his height. While everyone else was scrambling through last-minute notes, he sat in his chair looking unphased. Something about him made me want to talk to him.

"Hey," I said approaching him.

"Hey." He stood and smiled.

He had a nice smile. Nice lips even. Kissable lips. Okay, what was I thinking?

"I'm Sienna," I said. "I figured I should warn you that I'll be winning this competition."

He smirked. It was adorable. "I guess we'll see about that." Then a small frown creased his forehead. "Wait, your name is Sienna?" He stared at me for a moment like I was a math equation he was trying to solve, making my cheeks heat up under his gaze. Then he gave a small shake of his head and held out his hand. "It's a beautiful name. Nice to meet you. I'm Keene."

A Bottle of Sleep

The shop was dark. The air was so dry I could smell the dust that had drifted into corners like gray snow. And it was oven hot. I stood there, already feeling moisture beading on my forehead like the dryness was pulling it from me, and waited for my eyes to adjust.

"Hello?" My voice echoed, even though, as the dimness melted, I saw that the shop was crowded with...

What was it crowded with?

"Hello?" I called again. It had that empty feeling.

The opposite of being watched. I knew there was no one.

I took a step in, wondering if I should wait for the shopkeeper to return, and dust swirled up around my ankle. Then again, I wondered if there had ever even been a shopkeeper. My shirt was starting to stick to my underarms and I tugged at the long sleeves. I wished I'd brought an elastic for my hair.

What the shop was crowded with was shelves. They were made of old wood that looked like it would creak if I touched it. There was also an old counter with more shelves along the front, presumably where the shop's owner should be standing. I couldn't tell how large the place was because to either side of me, and behind the counter, were so many shelves I'd have to turn sideways to fit between them.

Each of the shelves was covered in what I assumed was drapes of cloth, though they were so gray they could have just been thick dust. A few remnants of cobwebs drifted off them, but even the cobwebs were old and tattered.

I shouldn't have been there. I should have stepped back out into the sunshine and forgotten about it.

But, now that my eyes were used to the gloom, I could see a faint glow coming from a spot on one of the shelves to my right. I took another step and coughed, not from the dust but from how dry the air was. It scraped at the insides of my nose and throat on the way down.

I got to the shelf and waited for the dust to settle around me. I felt so isolated in this place that the feeling turned eerie, like I should be able to watch my skin disintegrate as I stood there. Like time was either sped up or slowed way down, so that I was going to spend forever in this shop one way or another, and wouldn't be able to leave until I felt old enough to break.

I blew the dust off the glow, thinking I would take a look and get out.

But then I forgot what I had been thinking.

It was a jar. A plain old mason jar. And inside was... Well, it was something. And it was glowing. Soft yellow light washed over me, free from the eons of dust it had been buried beneath, turning and swirling. I could breath a little easier looking at it, like the light was bathing the air in freshness.

The longer I watched, the more content I became. The light was mesmerizing and soothing. It reflected off the things it was set next to, and I realized they were glass as well, though they didn't glow. I blew the dust off the thing to the right of the mason jar, and found a round blue bottle, about the size of my fist, with a flat base. The glass was dark, but I could see a sort of liquid inside. The bottle was topped with a small silver ball for a lid. Reaching up, I took the glass in my hand, lifting it off the shelf. It was cold and smooth. The liquid inside moved thickly and clung to the edges, like molasses. I could see my vague reflection in the dark blue glass, stretched so that my eyes were huge.

That was when I noticed a word etched into the silver lid: Sleep.

I peered at the bottle more closely. Maybe it was a medicine, or a poison. Even though I'd been holding the bottle for a moment, the glass was as cold as when I'd picked it up and I had to switch hands before it drained all the heat from one palm.

I reached to open the silver lid, when I saw something move in the reflection. And it wasn't me. I felt the chill from the bottle sweep down my arm and into my middle. I should not be here. I should leave. I felt it as sure as I could feel my heart beating. In the bottle's reflection, I could see something large moving behind me, yet I heard nothing. I felt nothing. There weren't any eyes prickling the back of my neck. There wasn't a faint hush of feet on floor. I felt alone, and yet I watched as a serpentine figure suddenly rose from behind me, mouth gaping, fangs reaching.

I whirled.

A man's smiling face was inches from me.

I shrieked and jumped back, crashing into the shelf behind me, upsetting all sorts of bottles, hearing glass clink as it tumbled into its neighbors.

The man reached an arm past my head and I flinched, but he only steadied the shelf.

His eyes never left me, even as the glass settled back into place and his hand retreated to fold itself with its pair in front of him. Large spectacles were pushed up close to his eyes, magnifying them. I supposed he was old, but it was hard to tell. He could have been anywhere from early thirties to late sixties. His hair was nondescript and pale, hard to tell if it was blonde or going white. It hung a little lank, almost reaching his shoulders.

"So," he said, drumming his folded fingers across his knuckles. "It seems you have found my shop." His voice was smooth. He was still smiling, looking at me expectantly, as though waiting for me to place an order.

I cleared my throat. "Yes?" It came out as a squeak. "Uh, yes. Sorry. I didn't mean to pry." I turned, though knowing he was looking at me with those enlarged eyes behind my back was unnerving, and shoved the blue bottle back into place. My own muffled reflection looked back at me from the bottle's surface and again, I could see in the reflection, a snake-like form behind me. Maybe it was a trick of the glass. I started when the image of the giant snake swerved around me, and leaned in on my left.

When I flinched away and looked to my left, there was the man, peering at me, smiling.

"I should go," I said, taking my hand away from the shelf and stepping back.

"But don't you want something before you leave?" he asked. "Isn't that why you came?"

My eyes flickered to the glowing mason jar. "Uh, no. That's all right."

He was suddenly closer.

I jumped back.

"I see you are fascinated with my jar of hope."

"Hope?" I asked.

"But perhaps the bottle of sleep is more suited to your needs?" He lifted the round bottle I'd been holding and weighed it in his palm, as though testing its durability. "After all," he said, "it is in sleep that we are our most lucid, our minds unlocked and unrestrained, able to make sense of the nonsensical and free to believe the improbable."

"The impossible, you mean."

He tipped his head, his smile coming back into place. "Ah. The impossible. Does it exist? Or does it only exist when we create it?"

I blinked. "Um, I need to be going. I have someone waiting for me."

His smile grew wider. "No one is waiting. If they were, you wouldn't be here, would you?" He set the bottle back in place.

I felt a chill run down my spine. "I was just curious."

"What are you curious for?" he asked. "What do you desire? You must long for something, or the jar of hope would not have drawn you in."

When I didn't answer, he leaned closer. "I have everything in this shop, bottled up safe, waiting for you to want it."

"Everything?" I asked.

He only smiled at me.

I peered at the shelves around me. There were all sorts of shapes and sizes, cloaked in dust, waiting to be revealed. "I don't want anything, but thank you." I felt I should take another step back. Turn, even, and walk out the door.

"Everyone wants something," he said. "Everything is wanted by someone."

"What if I don't know what I want?" I asked. I didn't mean to say the words. "Maybe I just wanted anything."

His smile curved up into his cheeks. "Isn't that why you're here? If you want something, it most likely wants you too."

I took a step forward, toward the shelf on my left, the one right up next to the counter. In my peripheral, I saw the man slide towards the back of the shop.

Nothing glowed on the shelf in front of me, so I blew the dust off a few shapes at random. They were all bottles. All glass. Though none of them were the same. One tall deep-green wine bottle was corked shut. A slip of paper tied around the bottleneck read: Jealousy. Next to it sat a squat square jar of clear glass. It was full to the brim with tarnished silver dust. A hammered metal label nailed to the shelf right below it said: Memory.

"Are these real memories?" I asked. None of this made sense, and yet, in a fluid sleep-like way, it almost did.

"Always ask the question you want to know the answer to," the man said, sliding behind the counter.

"Okay then. Where do you get all of these? These emotions and memories and things?"

"I buy as well as sell," he said. "People are always

24

happy to trade one thing for another. What they don't want, for what they do."

"So, if I bought these memories," I said. "Would they be the memories of the person who sold them to you?"

He folded his hands on top of the counter. "Well, they wouldn't be memories to you then, would they?"

I looked back at the jar of memory. "That doesn't make sense. How can you extract memory from one person and give it to another?"

"Everything makes sense, though not many people let the logic fall away far enough to understand. Unless they are asleep, of course."

I glanced across the room at the bottle of sleep.

Frowning, I moved past the counter and explored a new shelf, deeper in the shop, wiping dust from a glass sphere, almost like a crystal ball, except that inside was water. It looked like condensation, the way it collected on the inside of the sphere and ran down the edges, dripping from the top into a small puddle at the bottom. I watched it for a moment, wondering where the water came from. The puddle at the bottom of the sphere never got any larger, yet the water droplets kept forming and trickling down. I lifted it, and the water sloshed inside. When

I flipped it upside-down, the water collected at the bottom again, then formed on the sides and continued its endless cycle. There was no label.

"Sadness," the man said from right behind me, startling me so that I nearly dropped the glass ball. I set it down in the small grove that had been worn into the shelf for it. "Why would someone want sadness?" Selling it I understood, but not buying it.

"Oh, there are many reasons," the man said. "Some people feel they should grieve more for people who have passed on, people they were meant to love. Others have sold all their other emotions and need to erase the blankness left behind. Sadness is quite potent you know."

Beside the sphere of sadness was what looked to be an old-fashioned perfume bottle. When I blew the dust away, I was right.

"What is it you are looking for?" the man asked, his head sliding into my peripheral vision.

"Um..." The perfume bottle was made of cut crystal. It should have been grimy from sitting in the shop, but now that the dust was clear, the crystal sparkled, throwing off flecks of color and light. Etched into the metal around the spray part was: Happiness.

"I do want to be happy," I said, more for something to say. Then I gave an apologetic laugh. "But doesn't everybody?"

"You are not here for happiness," he said.

"Then what am I here for?"

He only smiled.

I looked back at the shelf, lifting something that looked delicate but was so heavy I almost I couldn't get it off the wood. When I dusted it off, it was a thin curved vase of blown glass, a startling rose color. Inside were gems roughly the size of pin heads. I guessed they were small diamonds, with a scattering of pearls. There was no lid, so I was careful not to spill them. In gold leaf on the shelf where I had lifted the vase away it read: Beauty.

I set it down carefully, feeling I should have been tempted. Beside it was a thin vial, lying on its side. Carved into the wood in jagged letters beside it was the word: Lust. When I wiped the dust away with a finger, I found that the black glass was sweaty, making the dust cling to it. The scent of blood reached me, and I pulled my hand away.

One more, I told myself. Just one more and then I have to go.

I walked past the shelf with Sadness and Beauty and Lust, and wandered, turning and picking out a shelf at random. The man watched me with amusement.

"You already know what you want," he said.

I took a deep breath, trying to ignore him, and picked out a lump on the shelf with my eyes. It made everything so much more tempting somehow, wrapping it in gray like a present, so you never knew what you would find beneath. As I stepped up to the shelf and reached for the shape, I could hear someone whispering. I turned, but the man was watching from where I'd left him, that same smile still on his face.

I reached for the shape again, lifting it. It was so light my hand shot into the air, expecting something heavier. The whispering got louder, as though it were coming from the shape itself. The hairs on the back of my neck stood up as I tried to make out the words in the hushed voices, but there were too many. The bottle was a flat square with a tarnished silver base and a tall thin cork of silver for a lid. The whispering got louder and angrier as I wiped the dust off the front of the glass. A swirl of red inside the bottle clarified into a face. A screaming, mouth-gaping human face. A piercing shriek made me drop the thing all together. The man was right beside me, and caught it before it fell.

I was shaking, my heart thumping inside me, my

palms slick. "What is that?" I asked.

"Fear," he said. "Strongest bottle I have." He slid it back into place on the shelf, and I turned away before I could make out any more faces in the red glass.

"I'm leaving," I said.

"You know what you want." He slid back into view.

I looked away from him, toward the front of the shop, but not at the door.

"You've known since you stepped inside." I shuddered and closed my eyes.

"You've wanted it for a long time. A very, very long time."

I squeezed my eyes shut, as though this could block out the sound of his smooth voice, slithering into my brain.

"You've wanted for so long, you are tired with wanting. You ache and yearn and bleed with it. And it's right here," he said. "It's sitting on that shelf, wanting you as much as you want it."

"No," I whispered.

"Take it," he said, his voice so close to my ear I should have felt his breath. "You can have it. The waiting can end. The wanting can end. It can all end. All go away. You just have to lift the bottle into your hands, one more time. Lift it, claim it, drink it. I know how very much you want to."

"Stop," I whispered. "I don't want it."

He laughed, low and smooth, like the laugh was just an exhale. "You want it so badly, you came into my shop. You want it so much, you would give anything, everything, to have it. Just look at it, sitting there, waiting for you."

I ducked my head and pressed my hands over my eyes. "No."

I could hear him slither around me, hissing, circling, waiting.

"You have been waiting for this for such a long time. And now it's yours. The waiting can have an end. Everything can have an end, if only you give into your want. Let your desire have you."

My breath was shallow and fast. "Please," I said. "Please, stop. I don't want it."

"No one will stop you," he said. "No one will care. You can do this. Everything is sitting in that glass bottle, and all you have to do, is step toward it."

The hissing grew louder in my ears.

"Think of it. Think of how it will be. This one final wish come true."

"I can't," I said.

"Oh, but you will. Desire has shaped you from the inside, carved you out until you have become your desire, until there is nothing left but desire. And the only satisfaction, the only contentment, is to fulfill it."

"That's a lie," I said, jerking my head up, forcing my eyes open.

His smile got wider. His teeth were jagged and sharp, two fangs sticking out over his lower lip. "You think you can escape what you want?" He slithered closer, his head weaving back and forth in front of me. "You are what you want. Every word, every glance, every breath."

"No," I said, my voice taking more substance. "I said I don't want it."

He hissed, sharp and warning.

"There might not be anyone waiting for me out there," I said, "but I am waiting for me. And I am more than this one want. I am stronger than this."

"You are this!" His eyes flashed, slitted pupils showing.

"No! I am so much more than this! I might want that one bottle, but I shouldn't want it. And I won't take it. I can still fight it. I can fight myself. And I can win."

The snake lunged for me, razor fangs barred, jaw

unhinged, ready to swallow me whole. I grabbed the nearest bottle and smashed it against the side of the snake's head, glass shattering, purple liquid dripping down my hand and into the snake's eyes. The liquid vaporized into thick smoke, and I darted for the door, coughing and trying to shake the stuff off my hand.

The snake caught my ankle and brought me crashing to the ground, my chin smacking the wood and making my teeth clack together.

I rolled onto my back, ready to fight, but the snake was gone. The rounded dark blue bottle rolled across the floor and bumped into my hand.

I looked at my reflection in it, eyes wide, mouth small.

My hand twitched.

Sleep.

I couldn't want it.

Was it Sleep for now? Or Sleep forever?

No. I didn't want it. Not really. Not for sure.

I jerked my hand away and I ran.

Especially Pink Daisies

Clarissa woke up coughing and thirsty.

The thirst burned down her throat and into her middle, dissolving her stomach, lungs, and heart. The coughs echoed inside her, she was so empty.

An adult lady with a tight bun beeped open a white door, spilling light into the dark room. The door had a square of glass to look through. The lady had a clipboard and a card on a lanyard around her neck. She was not Clarissa's aunt.

"Finally awake," the lady said, and scribbled on the clipboard. "How do you feel?"

Clarissa shrugged.

"I'm Ms. Stacey," the lady said.

From where she was lying on the bed, Clarissa looked around the room, but there wasn't anything to look at.

"And I see that you are Clarissa. Is that right?"

The room had a bed and a window and nothing else.

"Hmm." The lady shuffled to the window and looked through two layers of glass, one streaked with dried Windex. From the light in the hallway, Clarissa could see a window box hung on the sill with drying dirt and half-wilted flowers. She sat up.

"Hello," one of the flowers said in a high voice.

"Hello," Clarissa whispered. Her voice was hoarse.

"What did you say?" The lady turned.

"Nothing." Clarissa shook her head.

"Hmm." The lady wrote on her clipboard again. "Do you know why you're here, Clarissa?"

Clarissa shrugged.

The lady did more writing. "Your aunt brought you in yesterday. Do you remember that?"

Clarissa looked at the flowers.

"Your aunt is worried about you," the lady said.

The flowers were marigolds. Yellow, orange, and

red.

"Hmm." The lady tapped her clipboard. "Your aunt will be coming by soon. I'll send her in when she gets here." She left, clicking the door shut behind her.

Only a square of light from the door's window puddled into the room. Clarissa pulled her covers back. She was wearing a hospital gown. The floor was cold plastic tiles. Barefoot, she walked to the window.

"Are you still awake?" she asked the flowers.

"I'm thirsty," one of the orange-red marigolds said.

Clarissa nodded. "I'll find you some water."

But across the room, the white door didn't open. Even when she stood on tiptoe, she couldn't peek through the window at the top of the door. She tried the doorknob again. Then she went back to the flowers. The window didn't open either.

"I can't find any water," she said. Her throat felt extra scratchy and she blinked her eyes.

The flowers nodded in the breeze, and Clarissa folded her arms, leaning on the frame of the window. Her chest was starting to constrict, it was so empty.

"You look sad," a yellow marigold said.

Clarissa opened her mouth to breathe better. Her throat felt like it was closing. She swallowed. "I'm also thirsty," she said. The window was cold against her palm, and it made the glass fog around the edges of her fingers. When she took her hand away, there was still a hand-shape on the glass for one second.

The door behind Clarissa beeped.

"Clarissa?" A plump older woman with soft brown hair and round cheeks opened the door.

Clarissa didn't turn around.

"What are you doing at the window?" the woman asked.

"Nothing." Clarissa's voice was monotone. The whole room was monotone.

The woman looked at the flowers on the windowsill. Clarissa could see the woman's reflection in the dark window.

"Ms. Stacey told me you were up."

Clarissa breathed in and breathed out. Her breaths were shaky.

"I know things are hard right now, and I thought things would be easier for you here. I'll come in to see you whenever I can." The woman hesitated. "How are you doing?"

"Fine."

The woman looked at the door and around the

room, but there wasn't anything to look at.

"Dear," the woman said. "I've been thinking." The aunt took a few steps toward Clarissa, then stopped, still too far away to touch her. She looked around the room again. "Those are nice flowers," she said.

Clarissa looked down at the windowsill.

"What kind are they?"

"Marigolds." The paint was chipping where the windowsill met the glass.

"You know," the woman said. "Your mother loved flowers too, didn't she?"

Clarissa picked at the white paint.

The woman took a breath to speak, let it out, and then took it in again. "Sometimes, after a traumatic event, people will think things that aren't true. Did you know that?" She took another step forward. "I mean, after something bad happens, lots of people get confused. What do you think about that, Clarissa?"

Clarissa shrugged.

"Sometimes these people think something is good for them, when actually it's hurting them. Do you understand that, Clarissa?"

Clarissa shrugged again.

"It's hard to lose so much all at once. Do you

want to talk about it?"

"No."

"Alright," the woman let out her breath. "Well, I'll see you tomorrow." She retreated from the room and clicked the door shut behind her.

Clarissa looked up at the marigolds. "You'll be okay," she said.

"I'm thirsty," the yellow-red marigold said again.

Clarissa leaned her forehead on the glass. "Me too."

The long overhead light flipped on and Clarissa squinted.

"You're moving rooms." The lady with the card around her neck was back, but the clipboard wasn't.

Clarissa sat up in bed.

"Come on," the lady said, holding open the door. "It's down the hall. You'll be in a different section."

The hall was long and painted light yellow. The floor was brown carpet. The ceiling was fluorescent lights.

When they turned the corner, there was a room with two couches and low table with coloring books. And there were other kids. Maybe seven of them. A boy in a brown sweatshirt, jeans, and bare feet looked up as Clarissa and the lady walked by. He was maybe Clarissa's age, maybe a little older. His hair was brown and messy. He was coloring with crayons.

Clarissa's new room had no windows and no flowers. It did have a dresser and a little desk with a chair.

The lady opened the top drawer of the dresser and took out a stack of clothes.

"Your aunt brought these for you." She set the clothes on the bed.

Clarissa stood in the corner and watched.

"There are five shirts, two pairs of pants, seven pairs of socks, and seven pairs of underwear. I'll wait outside while you get dressed."

The lady left, closing the door behind her. The clothes were Clarissa's from home, but they felt strange. The jeans were stiff. The white t-shirt was loose. She didn't put on any socks.

The door wasn't locked this time.

The lady saw her when she opened it. "All done? It's time for breakfast."

Clarissa followed her out into the big room she'd

walked through before, with the couches and coloring books. All the kids were lining up, and Clarissa took the very end of the line. The boy with brown hair was in front of her.

"Hi," he said.

Clarissa didn't say anything.

The line moved down another hall to a tiny cafeteria. There were five tables, nine kids, and maybe ten grownups with them. All the adults had cards on lanyards around their necks.

Clarissa got a tray with bacon and scrambled eggs and hash browns. She sat down at the only empty table. But then the brown-haired boy sat down across from her.

"What's your name?" he asked. He had big brown eyes that made her not want to look at him, and then want to.

Clarissa looked around the cafeteria. The grown-ups were eating food too. One of them came over to their table. "Everything alright here?" he asked.

Clarissa and the boy nodded.

When the man left, the boy said, "I'm Leo."

"I'm Clarissa."

The boy nodded and picked up his fork for the scrambled eggs.

Clarissa rolled up a piece of bacon and poked it in her mouth.

"So what's wrong?" the boy asked.

Clarissa shrugged.

"Everyone has something wrong. I get sad. Really sad. And then sometimes I get scared. I tried to stay underwater at the pool until I stopped breathing, because I didn't want to be so sad anymore. That's when my mom brought me here. Sometimes she visits. Sometimes she brings me things, if the staff says it's okay. So, what's wrong with you?"

Clarissa said, "I'm thirsty."

The boy pushed his plastic cup of water over to her.

Clarissa shook her head. "Not that kind of thirsty."

The boy blinked his brown eyes. They were very brown.

Clarissa looked at the grown ups. Some of them were walking around the room. Some of them were sitting at the tables eating.

"I talk to flowers," Clarissa said.

"Because you're sad?"

"Sometimes."

The boy nodded. "What's your favorite flower?"

"All of them." She poked her fork at the scrambled eggs. "But especially daises."

"Which ones are daisies?" he asked.

"They have a big middle and lots of long petals around the edge. They can be any color you want, but I like the pink ones."

"Do they help you be happy?" the boy asked. "Pink daisies?"

"I'm not so thirsty when I look at them."

One of the adults clapped their hands. "Okay, everyone! Breakfast is over. Take your trays to the trash cans, put them on top, and line up."

"I don't think we have any daisies here," the boy said, standing up. "Not even outside."

The next morning, Clarissa didn't open her eyes when the light went on overhead. She was too tired to move. Too thirsty.

"Clarissa?" the lady with the bun said. "Clarissa, it's time to get up."

Clarissa coughed. "I'm sick," she said.

The woman left the room.

Clarissa wanted to go home. Her real home. She wanted her dad. She wanted her mom. She wanted sunshine and warm dirt and air that everyone else wasn't breathing. She wanted grass and moving clouds.

She wanted a flower.

The lady came back. "I've got a thermometer," she said. "I'm going to stick it in your ear. You'll hear a beep."

The thermometer tip was cold. There was a beep.

"Your temperature is fine," the lady said. "I don't think you're sick."

Clarissa coughed again. And she couldn't stop for a long time. Her whole body shook. When it passed, she kept her eyes closed. There wasn't anything to look at.

This was how they had both died – her mom and her dad. First the coughing.

"Clarissa," the lady said. "Look at me."

Clarissa kept her eyes closed.

"Clarissa, your aunt told me about this. You think you're sick, but you're not. Your brain isn't thinking right. Did your therapist talk to you about this yesterday?"

Clarissa thought about sunshine. She thought about daisies.

"Your parents were both sick. Is that right?" The lady waited. "You're scared that you'll get sick too. I understand that. But it's not true. The hospital tested you, and you don't have any of the germs your parents did. You're not sick, Clarissa."

Clarissa rolled onto her side, away from the lady.

"If you're not up in the next two minutes, you're going to miss breakfast."

A minute passed.

"I'll come back in an hour," the lady said. "If you're up and dressed, you can still have free time in the common room with everyone else."

The lady retreated, shutting the door and leaving Clarissa alone.

Clarissa shifted her weight. She coughed again.

When the lady came back, Clarissa hadn't moved.

She didn't open her eyes for the whole day.

She coughed and slept and woke and slept again, and never opened her eyes. Not even once. She buried herself in the covers.

She was so thirsty.

Thirsty enough to die.

That night, there was a tapping at her door.

She didn't move, but she listened.

The door opened.

"Clarissa?" the lady said. "Someone would like to see you."

Clarissa heard bare feet on the floor.

"Are you awake?" It was Leo.

Clarissa opened her eyes and pulled the covers off her face. The light was on in her room.

"I brought you something," Leo said. "Ms. Stacey said I could talk to you for a minute. She's right outside."

Clarissa sat up.

Leo held out a piece of paper with both hands. "I made this for you in free time today, because you weren't there. And I thought you might be sad like I am sometimes."

Clarissa took the paper. On it was a drawing of a bright pink daisy

A tear escaped, sliding down from the corner of her eye. She sniffed.

"Does it look like a daisy?" Leo asked. "I don't know if I did it right."

More tears were slipping out of the corners of Clarissa's eyes. She had to let go of the paper with one hand to wipe them all away. The tears dripped off her chin, and the tight feeling in her throat and chest let go.

"Do you like it?" Leo asked.

Clarissa nodded. "I don't feel so thirsty any-more."

Garlic in the Blood

The garlic plants were dead.

Sei knew before she pulled up the first bulb. She'd been trying to save them for weeks now as the stalks turned brown from the dirt up, wilting until they lay flat on the ground. She'd known they were dying. And now they were dead. All of them.

She had outlined her property in garlic, a line of plants poking out of the earth like bright green sentinels. And then she had planted another outline around her house. It was impossible to have too much. But this year there would be none at all.

Sei dropped the rotted bulb and wiped her palms on her jeans, smearing them with mud and decayed plant. More than the potatoes, more than the peas or the watermelon or the corn or even the wheat, Sei needed the garlic. She wouldn't have time to die of starvation if she ran out of garlic.

Wiping her sweaty forehead with the back of her hand, she got to her feet. The sun was low, sitting on the ground and glaring. It was time to drink her tea.

That was when she saw something she hadn't seen in over a year. A stranger.

At first, he was just a dark smear against the setting sun, but every muscle in her body from her little toes to her scalp tightened at the sight. People did not come and visit Sei. There wasn't a soul for miles. And there especially wasn't anything without a soul. At least, there shouldn't be.

And the garlic was dead.

She watched the man get closer. He was riding a horse of all things, which made her hunch her shoulders when she saw it, like she could make herself smaller, make herself disappear. She bent her knees like she was readying for a fight and her hand darted to her pocket where a long smooth piece of metal protruded. She was never without it, even after more than a year of solitude.

She swallowed hard, twisted her foot firmly into the dirt, and waited.

She watched him dismount, the horse throwing his head like he had been ridden too hard and too fast and was glad to be rid of his rider.

"Who are you?" she asked. Her voice was creaky from talking only to cats and chickens.

She saw him take in her stance, the metal stake in her fist. He raised his hands in surrender. "I'm Drake," he said. "I'm human."

"I can tell," Sei said. But she didn't relax her grip on the weapon.

"Are you Sei?" the man asked.

It was a stupid question. They both knew it, so Sei didn't answer.

The man – Drake – cleared his throat. "I need your help," he said.

"I'm done with all that." Sei narrowed her eyes. "So you can get right back on your horse and go back to where you came from."

"I can't!" Drake said. "There is no place to go back to anymore. It's gone." His voice cracked. "My whole village. It's gone."

Sei closed her eyes, trying to block out his words. "How many?" she asked.

"I think it's just one."

She snapped her eyes open. "One? That's impossible. How big is your village?"

"A few thousand. Or, it was. Only a couple dozen of us are left."

So it was small. But still.

"When did it start?" she asked.

"A month ago. It happened so fast, we didn't realize what was going on until it was too late."

Sei watched the rim of the sun slide out of sight. She couldn't be out here now.

"Male or female?" she asked.

"Does it matter?"

She waited for him to respond.

"Female."

"I can't," she said, turning away and striding across the garden toward her house.

"No!" Drake ran after her, grabbing her arm.

She turned on him, the metal stake raised. No one had touched her in years. Even before she retired, before she came to the farm and chose solitude over death, she was untouchable. People spoke to her with downcast eyes, keeping a safe distance, like she wasn't entirely human herself.

"I'm sorry," Drake said, dropping her arm and raising his hands again. The gesture irritated her.

She started back to her house.

"But if you don't help us, there won't be any of us left. My daughter-" His voice broke again.

It could all be an act. Sei knew this as she scuffed her boots off on the doormat and opened the front door. It could be a trap. There were plenty who wanted revenge on her. She just wasn't sure how they would have talked Drake – a human – into helping them.

"Did you get a good look at it?"

The man swallowed. "It looked young. We didn't realize at first. Not until it smiled. You know how it is."

"Hair?"

"Brown, kind of wavy, a lot like yours actually. And it had freckles. Cute little thing. Some of the men were looking her up and down until-" He looked down at his boots. "Why does it matter what it looks like?"

Sei flicked on the lights and turned to face him, her arms crossed. "I'm retired," she said. "You wouldn't want me anyway. I'm rusty by now. I haven't killed more than a chicken in fifteen months."

"You're the best there's ever been," he said. "And you're the only one left."

She turned away. "That's why I'm done," she said. "If I go back, I won't live any longer than the rest of you." Taking the kettle off the stove, she filled it with water from the tap and replaced it, turning on the burner and hearing the little drips of water on the outside of the kettle sizzle as the stove heated up. She opened the kitchen cupboard and took out her tea ball, a cluster of garlic cloves, and a ceramic dish of honey.

Drake watched her from the doorway, unmoving. As she made the tea, she avoided his eyes.

"I couldn't get within five miles of it anyway," she said and crushed the first garlic clove with the side of a butcher knife. The papery skin slid off and the sticky pale flesh went into the tea ball. She couldn't smell the garlic anymore. But she knew that Drake could. She was sure he could smell the farm – smell her – miles away. And he was only human.

"How often do you drink that?" Drake asked as she crushed the next clove and added it to the tea ball.

"More often than I eat," she said. "Eating is only important if you're going to be alive long enough to go hungry."

Drake looked around the kitchen, at the rows of braided garlic hanging from the rafters, at the sliver cross above the table, at the boxes of matches piled in a bowl next to the sink, at the hand-dipped candles standing on every flat surface, and at the gun on the window ledge. He could probably guess that the bullets inside were silver.

"When you eat garlic," she said. "It doesn't just stay on your breath. It gets into your system. It takes days to wear off."

She didn't just eat her garlic. She saturated her bath water with it, made lotion out of it, wore it in a locket that she never took off, stuffed her pockets with it, and made potpourri to fill her drawers.

She didn't just have garlic breath.

"I have garlic in my blood," she said.

Drake picked up the nearest candle and examined it. It too was full of dried garlic. He set it down.

"Why did you start?" he asked.

The kettle began to whistle. Sei pulled it off the stove with a hot pad and poured a steaming stream of water into her mug, dousing the tea ball full of juicy garlic cloves. She replaced the kettle and added honey to her mug.

"All those years ago," he said, "if you knew it was so dangerous, why start?"

She stirred the tea and looked out the window at the dark landscape. "Shut the door," she said. "And turn the locks. All of them."

Drake did as he was asked. She blew on her tea

to cool it but didn't take her eyes off the garden outside.

"It was my sister," she said. "She was a year younger than me."

She sipped the tea. It burned her tongue.

"She was killed right in front of me."

"I'm sorry," Drake said. "So you understand."

Sei set down her mug with a hard clink. "Her murderer was my first kill."

Drake met her hard gaze with his own. "Not all of us can do that," he said. "You have a talent. A gift."

"I have a curse," she said. "They may not have souls, but each and every one of them haunts me to this day." She felt herself breathe in. Made herself hold it, lungs full, trying to block the memories. "Two hundred twenty seven," she said when at last she exhaled.

Drake took in his breath.

No one realized how many it was. She had a scar for each and every one of them. A physical scar, either from their nails, or from their teeth, or from the fire when she burned their bodies. Fights were messy. Fights left wounds. But nothing on her body was as permanent as the scars on her mind. Teeth and fire and blood could never do as much damage as a memory.

"What would your sister want?" Drake asked.

It wasn't a fair question, and they both knew it.

She gazed out the window even though it was too dark to make out much but the line between the black ground and the star speckled sky.

The garlic was dead.

She turned away from Drake, putting her hands on the countertop and closing her eyes.

"Give me a week," she said.

Drake inhaled to speak, but she cut him off.

"That's the best I can do. Even after a week of detox, I'll still have garlic in my blood." She would have to sweat it out, move away from this farm that had garlic in the very wood the house was built from. A week wasn't even close to enough time.

It was suicide and she knew it.

But she had known this was coming. Known it since her first kill. And what else was there?

There were the chickens and the cats. There was the garden. There was life. There was the simple pleasure of breathing in and out.

But how high a price was she willing to pay for those simple things? Would she give up her sister again? Would she give up this man's daughter?

"One week," she said. "And then I'll go after my sister."

Milk with Honey

What scared her most wasn't that she heard the voices.

Rob is pulling into the driveway.

She wasn't scared of being insane.

Rob parked the car on the left side of the garage.

She wasn't even scared of people knowing she was insane.

Rob is walking around to sit on the front porch.

What scared her was that the voices might be right.

Rob is thinking about you.

If they were, she didn't want to know.

She watched Rob open the front door, glance at her, and go into the kitchen.

Rob wishes you had left some dinner for him.

Pushing off the couch, she climbed the stairs to the second floor. Being in the same room as him was like trying to breathe through a pillow.

Rob is microwaving left over mac and cheese.

She turned on the shower to drown out the voices. After soaking in the hot steam for almost an hour, the heat ran out so she shut off the water. She pulled on a baggy t-shirt and sweatpants and crawled under the covers, trying to warm the space by herself.

Rob is taking a cold shower downstairs.

She clicked off the bedside lamp and buried herself under the covers, listening to herself breathe.

Rob is thinking of you.

Sleep was a like a finicky cat she tried to coax into coming closer. She dreaded the night. Dreaded this pillow. This comforter. This bed. Sleep and her had always had a wary relationship. A relationship that had only gotten worse in the past two weeks.

Ever since the voices started.

Rob is still awake.

She pulled the pillow out from under her head and slapped it over her head, like the voices were a sound she could block out.

Rob is going into the kitchen to microwave a mug of milk.

For just a moment, she let the pillow flop to the side as she remembered sitting on the kitchen counter in pink button-up pajamas, cradling a mug of milk in her hands, leaning into Rob in his gray t-shirt that still smelled of cologne.

She shook her head and pulled the covers all the way up over her.

Rob picked the blue mug.

Her favorite one.

Rob has the milk out and is standing there, looking at it.

She flung the covers off and swung her legs out of bed. Maybe she should take another shower. It would be cold, but maybe that would help.

Rob poured the milk and put it back in the fridge.

She could picture him, standing there in those striped pajama pants that were too long, the ones she was going to hem months ago.

Rob entered one minute and thirty seconds into the microwave.

She pressed her palms against her ears and hummed as loud as she could. Until she realized she was humming a love song.

Rob took the blue mug out of the microwave and added honey.

She had forgotten about adding honey. That was the best part. He said honey was good for her voice. Her beautiful, honeyed voice, he said, that had got stuck in his head more than any love song.

Sometimes he had still tasted like honey when he would kiss her on those nights.

Rob only took one sip. He left the rest untouched.

Picking up her pillow, she flung it across the room, hitting the dresser with a poof. She retrieved it and then stood still in the middle of her room, the pillow dangling from one hand. The voices were quiet. Maybe they were done talking for the night.

She scooted back into bed, avoiding the left side, and focused on her breathing.

Rob is still thinking about you.

2:00 am. Sleep wasn't around to even be tempted into taking her.

She stared at the alarm clock across the room. Rob used to turn the alarm off in his sleep, until she moved the clock off his bedside table and to the dresser.

Rob is asleep in the basement, she imagined the voices saying, but they were quiet.

She wandered down the stairs and stared at the microwave clock instead. It read 0:13. He hadn't let the microwave timer run out. He always used to do that, trying to get it to stop on her lucky number.

Rob can't sleep. He's thinking about you.

She hit the microwave's end button.

Rob is looking at you. He doesn't want to wake you.

Her eyes blinked open, taking a sleepy second to adjust. Rob blinked as well. In that small moment of time before her memory rebooted, she thought he was going to kiss her and climb into bed. His kiss would taste like honey.

Then she blinked again, and he turned away. She remembered him shouting, yelling, screaming.

She remembered twisting off her ring and flinging it at him. She remembered him driving away. She had put his toothbrush and shampoo in the basement bathroom and untangled their dirty clothes in the hamper, dumping his on the downstairs bed. When he got home late that night, he had gone to her, tried to wrap her in his arms and kiss her forehead, but she had stepped away. That was two weeks ago.

Looking blearily around, she realized she was lying on the sofa with a quilt from the basement tucked in around her. She remembered being in the kitchen and then sitting on the couch to think. She'd obviously fallen asleep, though she didn't remember that part. She pushed herself up, bundling the quilt around her shoulders, and climbed the stairs.

Rob can't stop thinking about you.

She got up early and turned on the oven.

The cookies were oatmeal and had whole-wheat flour, so that had to count for something. But still, they were cookies. And this was supposed to be breakfast.

Rob is awake.

She glanced up with oven mitts on both hands

as Rob pushed open the basement door, yawning. His hair was sticking straight up on one side and his cheek was indented with sleep lines. Then he saw her.

Rob didn't know you were awake yet. He was going to cook bacon and eggs for breakfast.

She turned away to get the milk from the fridge. He could cook all the bacon and eggs he wanted. She wasn't stopping him.

Rob was going to leave half for you.

She put the cookies on a plate.

Rob is watching you. He wonders if he's allowed to eat a cookie.

She wasn't hungry anymore.

Rob wants to ask you a question. He wants you to turn around.

She stood with the plate of cookies in her hands, looking at the counter and thinking about setting the plate down. But that was when she saw the dishes spilling out of the sink and onto the countertops. When did they pile up like that? One cup was tipped over and orange juice had puddled around a stack of plates with dried spaghetti sauce stuck to them. When did they eat spaghetti? She couldn't remember.

Rob really wants you to look at him.

She bumped a pot out of the way with her el-
bow and set the cookies down. When she tried to
adjust the plate, it was stuck in something sticky. If
she turned around, she might see him looking at her.
She might know that the voices were right. About
everything.

Rob decided it would be safer to have cereal.

She busied herself with moving dishes around,
arranging them in piles and then rearranging them.
She should wash them today. Why had she not noticed them for so long?

Rob wants a bowl and you are in the way.

She turned without thinking. He was a step behind her. She could smell his left-over body wash.

He cleared his throat.

She skittered away before he could speak and
ran for the upstairs shower, flushing her skin with
scalding water, but she wasn't fast enough.

Rob is thinking about you.

She called in sick to work. Then she ran a bath
for herself and lay on her back, her ears submerged,
listening to the strange murmuring of the water. She
couldn't make out any words. When the bath went

cold, she drained it and ran it again.

Rob is pulling into the driveway.

She started, splashing water over the side of the tub. She climbed out, slipping on the tile floor and grabbing the sink. It was only 4:00 pm. He usually didn't get home until after 5:00.

Rob parked the car on the left side of the garage.

They used to pretend to fight over the right side of the garage, the side closer to the house, seeing who could get home from work first and claim it. Her car was parked in the driveway now since she'd been carrying in groceries last time she parked, and the garage didn't lead into the house. The right side was open. He could have parked there.

Rob is walking around to sit on the front porch.

She toweled off and changed into something re-sembling awake clothes and crept down the stairs to look out the front window. Rob was sitting on the front porch steps, looking up at the sky. She didn't need the voices to tell her, but they did anyway.

Rob is thinking about you.

She sat on the couch with an open book and thought about climbing back into her tepid bath.

Rob is coming inside.

She jumped as she heard the front lock slide open. Rob's tie hung loose. His hair was standing on end, and his eyes were tired. She could picture him running his hands through his hair, making it stand up just like that. She remembered how she used to run to him as soon as he walked through the door, throwing herself into his arms. On days when his tie would be loose, she would laugh and undo it the rest of the way. He didn't even glance at her as he plodded toward the kitchen.

She startled herself by asking, "Everything all right at work?" Probably it was just habit, seeing his loosened tie. She didn't mean anything by it.

He blinked and focused on her, like she had gone a little transparent.

"Yeah. It's fine."

He kept looking at her until she turned away and ran up the stairs. But she didn't get into the bath. She drained the water and sat in the wet bathtub and listened for the voices. But they didn't say anything.

When it was starting to get dark outside, she tiptoed to the kitchen. He wasn't in sight, so she sat on the edge of the counter and nibbled at a cookie, but didn't get out any milk. Then that she realized there was space to sit on the counter. The dirty dishes were gone.

Rob is lying on the bed downstairs, looking at the ceiling.

Rob misses you.

She pulled her feet up onto the counter and leaned back against the cupboard, wrapping her arms around her legs. The cookie was making her feel sick.

Rob is climbing the basement stairs.

Her arms tightened around her knees. She stared at the floor so hard she could see that it had been swept.

When the basement door opened, she didn't move. She felt strange knowing he was standing in the doorway, looking at her. She didn't need the voices to tell her that. She thought about sitting in that empty bathtub and how it had felt like they matched, her and the tub.

Rob is looking at you.

She lifted her face just enough to see him. His arms were crossed over his chest, but not in defiance. It looked more like self-preservation. He dropped his gaze when she met it.

Rob doesn't want to be hurt any more.

Neither did she. But she was already so hurt inside that maybe it didn't matter anymore. Maybe once you were empty and wet and drained, nothing mattered.

He cleared his throat. "I'm packing up my stuff."

He waited a minute, not meeting her eyes. "I'll be out by tomorrow."

The words tightened around her throat like he had choked her with them. She had already lost him. She had lost him two weeks ago. And she had been getting more lost every day, wandering around inside her head, trying to drown herself in hot water.

Rob doesn't want to lose you.

She was losing him anyway. It didn't matter if it had already happened or was about to. It didn't matter what either of them wanted. It had happened. Or was happening. It would be over soon.

Rob wants you to say something to him.

Rob turned back to the basement stairs.

Rob wants you to stop him.

"Rob?" Her voice came out shaky. She realized she hadn't said his name the whole two weeks.

With that one word, the voices in her head went silent. The steady hum she hadn't even known was there, faded away. She was on her own.

He didn't answer, but she knew he was listening, staring down those dark steps that would lead him away for good.

"Rob," she said again. "Do you want some warm milk?"

When he still didn't respond, she realized how

badly she wanted him to say "yes." Wanted him to come and wrap his arms arounds her, curled up there on the counter, knees and all, like he used to.

"Rob?" Her voice, her heart, her whole self was close to cracking. "I don't want you to leave."

He didn't move.

"I'm sorry, Rob. I'm so sorry. This is all my fault. I'm sorry. I'm sorry. I'm-" She broke. It was too late. He would be gone in the morning and he would never ever come back.

Tears ran down her cheeks, filling the void that had been aching inside her. She put her head on her knees and sobbed.

"Rob, don't go. Please, don't go." She untangled her limbs and fell off the counter onto her feet, gulping down the sobs, moving toward Rob's frozen form. Placing a trembling hand on his back, she leaned her head on his shoulder. He didn't react.

"I still love you," she whispered, sliding her arms around him.

It seemed much more than minutes that she stood there, hanging onto the man who was still her husband, at least for one last moment.

His lungs exhaled. Then slowly, carefully, he took in a breath.

"With honey?"

Rip Tide

My legs break.

I scream, the sound garbled, the last of my air scattering in bubbles.

Slices of pain crack down my thighs and calves. Water under and above me. In my ears, in my hair, in my mouth.

I thrash.

My fingers throb. My neck sears and I clutch my throat. Air. I need air.

My legs bump against each other and stick, like they're coated in honey. I try to pull them apart, but the stickiness on them turns to wet cement and hardens, locking them together.

And still, I can't reach the surface. I can't think. I can't swim. I can't breathe.

I claw at the sunlight out of reach, shimmering through the water.

It's too far. I'm too deep.

My feet spasm.

I am dying.

My lungs are full and heavy, but not with oxygen. My whole body is writhing and twisting. The water burns my skin.

My legs begin to bend. Unnatural. Not at the knees. In the middle of my thighs. At the bottom of my calves. My bones feel shattered.

I need air. I clamp my mouth shut. I will not drown. I will not drown.

I am drowning.

My legs twist, all bends and breaks, like the bones in them have become spines, my knees no longer an anomaly.

My neck flares with pain and I feel cuts slice through my skin under my fingers.

My lungs scream and scream, and pull and pull. From the center of my lungs, a sensation knifes through me, down each limb, into each finger and toe, making me jerk.

And then I drop, limp, weighed down, and broken.

I thump against the sandy sea floor, limbs sprawling, legs curled sideways, stuck together. For a moment, the knifing sensation washes over me in waves, thrumming inside me, still pain but not quite so exquisite. I don't want to surrender. I don't want to drown.

But every cell in my body feels so far away and slow, like the sensation is weight and maybe nothing more. I feel myself fading into it, and then it settles on me like silt.

The pain fades, and I blink, waking from it, like the pain was a drug.

I exhale. Inhale water.

I am still underwater.

Exhale.

Water rushes down and around my neck. I put my hands up and feel the slits there, just under the back of my jaw.

Inhale.

I am underwater. I am breathing.

I am breathing underwater.

Exhale.

I have gills.

Inhale.

I have gills!

Exhale.

Why do I have gills?

And then I see my fingers. Light from above is swirling off them, twisting, reflecting the sea's mood above me. The light makes me look pale. But my fingers are not just pale. They are webbed.

I try to shake off the ribbons that connect finger to finger, They are pliable but unyielding. They catch the water. I shake harder, breathe faster.

I must already be dead.

In between worlds.

Asleep.

I must be going crazy.

The lack of air is making me see things before I die. I've spent too long obsessing over sea life, and now my brain is mixing it with reality. I am experiencing brain damage as I go longer and longer without air.

I inhale deep again. Inhale water. And exhale it through my gills.

Then I see the sea creature beside me. I yelp in surprise, bubbles escaping my mouth.

I scoot back, trying to get away from its long eel-like form, but it comes with me. And then I see. It's not a creature. It's me. It's my legs.

They are slimy, sand griming them. They are stuck together, the slime hardening, but bendable. And they are broken. They must be broken.

Legs don't bend like that.

Fish bend like that. Eels bend like that. Not legs.

They are twisted and curved, like they were mangled and dropped. But there is no pain left in them.

I must be dying.

And my feet. My feet are flat, toes splayed. They're slimy too. My toes are webbed like my hands. And they're broken too, toe joints separated from each other, toes long and inhuman. As I watch, the slime is building itself around my toes, collecting on them and hardening. I flick my feet and the slime slides down them further, hardening at the tips like icicles or stalactites dripping and growing. The slime is so repulsive that I can't look away.

This is not my body.

I no longer know what is reality and what is imagination or hallucination.

All I know is, I have a tail. A fish tail. With fins forming off my feet. I kick my legs again, feeling dizzy at the way they ripple, like the bones in my legs were sectioned into vertebra.

I have gills. I have webbed fingers. I have a tail. I pass out.

That first breath of air feels insubstantial. My lungs lift inside me, expecting weight to fill them, and I bob in the water. I can breathe!

The night is black. I make out the shore in the distance and swim for it, my legs or tail feeling awkward and unsure. I don't want to bend my legs, don't want to feel how they move. But I can't swim without them.

When I crawl onto the beach, I realize I am naked and shivering. Shredded pieces of my swimsuit cling to my shoulders. I think the slime that coats my legs ate away at the fabric. But I don't know. I don't know anything.

I don't want to know anything. I want to pass out again.

I lay with my cheek pressed to the sand, waves washing over me, and breathe normal breaths. I wonder if I am still alive, or if this is after life and it only feels the same but isn't.

Then I look around, and see a beach house in front of me. Our house. Three abandoned towels are sitting out. I drag myself to the biggest one, bleached white, and try to wrap it around me because even if this is the afterlife, I still appreciate clothing. But my legs are stuck to each other making standing impossible, so I have to roll myself up in the towel like a burrito, leaving my arms out to adjust me.

Then I lay there and breathe, and touch my neck with my strange hands. The gills are still there, but closed now, flat against my neck. Only small little ridges show where they are.

"Help," I say, and my voice rasps, my throat coated in salt. I cough and swallow. "Help. Help me!" My voice is hoarse.

I flip onto my stomach and try to crawl toward my house, but with my legs stuck together, and the towel dragging in the sand, my arms aren't strong enough.

"Help!" I say again, louder.

The porch light flips on. The screen door squeaks open.

And I wish I hadn't said anything, because what will my parents say when they see me? Will they see me? Maybe I exist in an alternate dimension. Maybe I am dead and only a ghost.

I hear feet on the wooden steps.

"Cindy? Oh my gosh! Cindy!" Natalie, my older

sister, runs down the beach toward me.

"Don't panic," I say. "I think..." My voice is scratchy. "I think I'm evolving into an aquatic animal. But I also think I might just be hallucinating." I kick my legs to make my point, and the hardened slime trailing off my toes breaks off. Encouraged that the transformation might not be permanent, I kick my legs harder and wiggle them against each other, trying to force them apart.

Natalie is still standing, staring at me.

I sit up and touch my legs for the first time since any of this began. They are dry and scaly. The slime flakes off in my hands. Rubbing at my legs, big chunks of it break off and disintegrate into the sand. When I pull my legs in opposite directions, there is a crackling noise and then they break apart from each other.

My heart flies up in my chest, thinking I've just broken off a piece of my leg, but no. My legs are all there, separate. They ache like I've exercised them too hard and pulled a muscle. I can feel the bones inside groaning and pulling together. I sit back on my hands, the towel still tucked tight around me, and wiggle my toes. Even my feet are looking more normal. More human. I hold up one hand, and then rub between my fingers with my other hand. The webbing comes off, dry and dusty.

I breathe in, and let my breath out in a whoosh.

I am human. I am still human.

I don't know what just happened in the water. I don't know if I lost consciousness and imagined it all, hallucinated it as I fought for air.

I don't know, and I don't want to know. I shift a leg and it bends at the knee, all proper and straight. I collapse back on the sand.

"Cindy?" Natalie asks.

I'd forgotten about her.

"It's okay," I say. "It's going to be alright. It was nothing. Just a little sea slime that got on me while I was swimming."

"Here," she says, crouching down to put an arm under my shoulder and help me to my feet.

I feel unsteady on my legs, like Ariel the first time on land. But no. Nothing like that. I've always been human. Always will be.

"You were gone for so long. We tried to find you. What happened to your swimsuit?"

I shake my head.

"Let's get you inside."

Natalie gets me some pajamas while I lock myself in the bathroom and shower the last of the slime cement off my legs. They're normal legs. Human legs.

My legs.

When I get out of the bathroom, Natalie has poured us each a bowl of cornflakes, but I'm not hungry.

"You okay?" she asks, sitting down next to me at the table.

"I don't know," I say. Then I wish I hadn't, because it makes me sound crazy and desperate. I take a bite of cornflakes and make myself chew.

"You want to talk about it?" Natalie asks.

I don't answer, because shaking my head makes it seem like a big deal, but I can't say anything. She'll think I'm insane.

"It was nothing," I say. "I was snorkeling and got too far out. A current caught me and pulled me under. I thought I was going to drown."

"That sounds pretty scary," she says. "How'd you make it out?"

I shrug. "I swam."

"Diagonal to the rip tide?" she asks.

"Yeah, I guess. That's the only way to get out, right? I got lucky."

"That's so freaky. You should take a buddy next time. Especially at night."

"Yeah. I guess so. But it turned out alright." I sip my cornflake milk and hand the bowl back to her, still full.

"I'd better get some rest," I say. "I'm pretty tired."

"Okay. Good idea," Natalie says. "Get some rest."

I make myself smile and stand. "See you tomorrow."

The next morning I'm up early, before anyone else. I didn't sleep.

I get the kayak out of the garage and drag it out to the water with a paddle and a life vest. I push out into the water and climb in at the last second, my toes pushing off the sand. I row hard and fast, still tired but awake.

When I get out far enough that no one on shore can see me, I take off the life vest, clip it to the oar, and lock the oar into place on the side of the kayak.

Then I strip to my underwear. I'd really like to have clothes to put back on after this is over.

I stand, wobbling in the boat, arms outstretched, and eye the water. Then I jump.

The water enfolds me, wraps around me and makes my neck tingle.

I open my eyes.

My mouth is shut tight, air trapped in my lungs,

turning me into a bubble. I bob in the water.

The water is so blue and clear, light making patterns, caught in the folds of H2O molecules. I look over at the little boat and I hold my hands up to examine them. They are just hands.

I swim up a little and touch the boat, one hand on the side, head still underwater.

I try to open my mouth, but my brain overrides me, instinct kicking in.

My mouth is sealed shut, locking in the air I need to live. The air my brain thinks I need. I tell my brain that it came up with this idea in the first place. That if it doesn't work, I can lift my head out of the water in a second. That I won't drown. But my brain is having none of it.

Finally I come up for air and climb into the boat, dripping and cold. I wrap my arms around my legs.

I can't do this. What if it works? What if it doesn't work? What if it's irreversible? What if it was a one time thing? What if I'm crazy?

But I have to know. I have to know or the unknown will suffocate me, drown me in the undiscovered. This is me. This is my body. My life.

I have to know.

Gritting my teeth, I slide over the edge of the boat again, sinking underwater.

I close my eyes, shut down my brain. Drown out everything but the lull of the water against my skin, rocking me, swaying me with the tide.

I open my mouth and breathe in.

Soray and the Monster

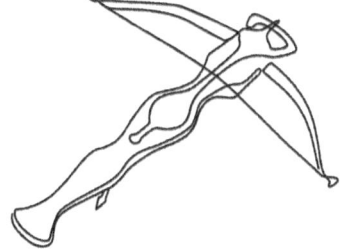

Once upon a time, there was a monster and there was a girl. The girl's name was Soray, and she was fifteen years old. The monster didn't have a name, not a real name anyway.

Once upon a time, there were monsters everywhere. Monsters with teeth and claws. Monsters that could hide anywhere, be anything.

Once upon a time, a monster and a girl met in the forest. Or maybe it was a boy and a girl. It was always hard to tell with monsters. The boy had an ax. The girl had a basket and her mother's crossbow.

Inside the basket were two pats of fresh churned butter, one jar of strawberry jam, and a bouquet of wild honeysuckles. Inside the crossbow was an arrow. The basket was for her grandmother who lived in the forest because she wasn't afraid of the monsters. The crossbow was for staying alive.

When Soray was seven, a stranger knocked on the door, and her father let him inside. The snow was as deep as Soray's shoulders and the stranger was shivering so hard he was making his own windstorm inside their cottage. Her father gave him a blanket by the fire, but before the tea was hot the stranger had thrown off his disguise and had eaten her father in three dripping bites. The monster had more teeth than Soray could count. It would have eaten her too if her mother hadn't shot it through the head.

Monsters were everywhere.

When the boy and the girl saw each other, the boy dropped his ax and Soray dropped her basket and her bow. The honeysuckles and the jam and the butter spilled out. The crossbow hit a rock, springing the arrow and almost hitting the boy.

"I'm not a monster," the boy said.

"I don't believe you," Soray said. That was her last arrow. "Only monsters live in these woods."

"You're here," the boy monster said.

"I'm visiting my grandmother."

"Is she a monster?"

Soray narrowed her eyes. "No. She's a fool."

She could grab the crossbow. But she didn't have any more arrows. She didn't know how long it would take to run to her grandmother's house. And she knew there was no one else nearby to hear her scream.

So instead of shooting, or running, or screaming, she knelt down and gathered up her honeysuckle bouquet. Some of the flowers had fallen off, but she swept them into the basket anyway. The butter's cloth was dirty, but she brushed it off. The jam jar was fine.

"If you're going to eat me," she said, "I can't stop you."

"I'm not going to eat you," the boy said.

Soray put the crossbow on her back. "Good. Because my grandmother would find you and shoot you if you did."

"Where does she live?" the boy asked. He still hadn't picked up the ax. But monsters didn't need axes to eat people.

"I'm not telling you," said Soray.

The boy looked at her basket. "There are more

honeysuckles just off the path." He pointed.

Soray didn't look where he was pointing. If she turned, he might change into something with too many teeth and then it would be too late. Maybe it was already too late.

"Why do you have an ax?" she asked.

"In case I meet any monsters." Hefting the ax handle, he unstuck the blade from where it had buried itself in the ground.

Soray took a step back. "I'm going to go find my arrow."

The boy nodded and put the ax on his shoulder. "Okay."

Soray waited for him to move. When he didn't, she sucked in her breath and marched past him, stepping off the path and into the tangled vines. She didn't look back to see if she was going to be eaten.

When she found the arrow, it was embedded in a tree trunk so deep she couldn't get it free. When she turned around, the boy was gone.

Her grandmother's cottage was small with a vegetable garden out front. When Soray knocked on the door, she heard her grandmother shuffle to open it, lifting the latches that kept it locked one by one.

Her grandmother was wearing a floured apron, and her house smelled like fresh bread. The aroma made Soray's mouth water. She held out the basket.

"My mother wanted me to bring you these, grandmother."

"Come inside, child. Come inside." Her grandmother ushered her in and closed the door, doing the latches back up, one by one.

Soray set the basket on the table. Her grandmother's crossbow wasn't by the door. Neither were her arrows. "Where are your arrows?"

Her grandmother shuffled to the table, rubbing her back. "I ache something fierce today," she said. "Let's see what your mother sent." Lifting the honeysuckles, she peered in at the butter and jam. "How thoughtful."

Soray backed away. "Grandmother," she said. "Where is your crossbow?"

"Why ever are you asking about it, child?" Her grandmother set the jam on the table with a hollow thunk.

"I need a new arrow," said Soray. "For my trip back home. There are monsters in these woods, you know."

"Yes," said her grandmother. "Yes, there are."

Soray narrowed her eyes. "I'm hungry," she said. "May I have something to eat?"

"Of course." Her grandmother smiled. Her teeth

were sharp. "I'm hungry too."

Soray ran for the door, but the monster got there first, all resemblance to her grandmother gone. Only the apron stayed tied around the monster, drool dripping onto it.

Soray knew it was foolish, but she screamed anyway. Grabbing the jam off the table, she threw it at the monster and ran for her grandmother's bedroom, slamming the door closed behind her. There on the bed sat the crossbow and a quiver of arrows. Shucking the crossbow off her back, she slid an arrow free and notched it.

The door banged open, hitting the wall. The boy from the forest was standing there. The ax was gone.

Soray leveled the crossbow at him.

"I'm not a monster," he said.

"I wish I believed you." Soray pulled the trigger.

Love this Book?

I would appreciate it if you could take a second to leave a review. Reviews help authors, especially indie authors, to get their book noticed. Scan the QR code below to leave a quick review!

Acknowledgments

Thank you to everyone who made this book possible! These stories were previously published on my writing blog (which no longer exists) and I am so grateful to everyone who read that blog and commented on it. It kept me going for a long time! Thank you to my advance readers who made this book the best it could be! Lastly, thank you to you, reader, for picking up this book and sticking with it to the end. Short stories are my favorite thing to write, and I am so grateful for the opportunity to share my best ones with you!

About the Author

IZI MILLER has a Bachelor's degree in English from Brigham Young University and a Masters of Library and Information Science from Valdosta State University. She and her adorably nerdy husband live in Idaho with their black cats, Cinder and Nico. She loves mermaids, pink diasies, and warm milk with honey.

www.izimiller.com
izimillerauthor@gmail.com